REACHING FOR THE STARS

BRINGING SPACE HOME

Mike Downs

ROURKE'S
SCHOOL to HOME
CONNECTIONS

BEFORE AND DURING READING ACTIVITIES

Before Reading: *Building Background Knowledge and Vocabulary*

Building background knowledge can help children process new information and build upon what they already know. Before reading a book, it is important to tap into what children already know about the topic. This will help them develop their vocabulary and increase their reading comprehension.

Questions and Activities to Build Background Knowledge:

1. Look at the front cover of the book and read the title. What do you think this book will be about?
2. What do you already know about this topic?
3. Take a book walk and skim the pages. Look at the table of contents, photographs, captions, and bold words. Did these text features give you any information or predictions about what you will read in this book?

Vocabulary: *Vocabulary Is Key to Reading Comprehension*

Use the following directions to prompt a conversation about each word.

- Read the vocabulary words.
- What comes to mind when you see each word?
- What do you think each word means?

Vocabulary Words:

- *ablative*
- *prosthetics*
- *reconnaissance*
- *robotics*
- *space blankets*
- *technology*

During Reading: *Reading for Meaning and Understanding*

To achieve deep comprehension of a book, children are encouraged to use close reading strategies. During reading, it is important to have children stop and make connections. These connections result in deeper analysis and understanding of a book.

Close Reading a Text

During reading, have children stop and talk about the following:

- Any confusing parts
- Any unknown words
- Text-to-text, text-to-self, text-to-world connections
- The main idea in each chapter or heading

Encourage children to use context clues to determine the meaning of any unknown words. These strategies will help children learn to analyze the text more thoroughly as they read.

When you are finished reading this book, turn to the next-to-last page for **After-Reading Questions** and an **Activity**.

TABLE OF CONTENTS

Gadgets Galore 4
Hot and Cold 16
Preventing Problems 22
Food for Thought 26
Diagram of NASA's Mars Perseverance Rover 30
Index 31
After-Reading Questions 31
Activity 31
About the Author 32

GADGETS GALORE

Space is in the news! Rockets launch hundreds of satellites every year. Astronauts visit the *International Space Station (ISS)* regularly. The National Aeronautic Space Administration's (NASA's) Mars 2020 Perseverance mission captured thrilling footage of its rover landing in Mars' Jezero Crater on February 18, 2021. It's amazing! But if you're not an astronaut, how does any of this affect you?

You might be surprised! Inventions needed to explore space have already changed our lives. And new inventions will continue to do so. Space **technology** has improved everything from tennis shoes to cell phone cameras, from eyeglasses to firefighting gear.

technology (tek-nah-luh-jee): the practical application of knowledge in a specific field, such as space

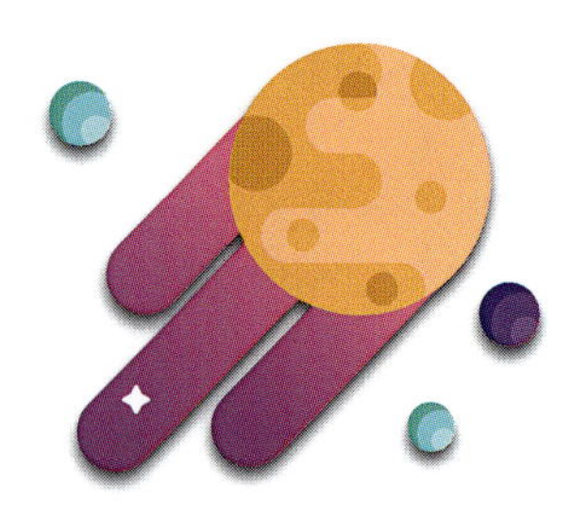

Many of these inventions focus on making things small. There is not much room on a spacecraft. In the 1990s, scientists knew they needed smaller cameras to use in space. These cameras also had to take amazing pictures. And that is how we developed the technology that led to cell phone cameras. Now millions of people around the world use this technology to take pictures of everything from selfie pictures with their friends to breathtaking photos of the world.

Catching Crooks

Scientists invented new technology to improve jittery space videos. This technology helps the Federal Bureau of Investigation (FBI) identify criminals with clearer videos and pictures.

"Okay, Houston, we've had a problem here."

This famous quote from the Apollo 13 mission shows how important good communication is. During the Apollo 13 mission, communication saved the astronauts' lives. Astronauts can't hold a microphone on a spacewalk. They need both hands free when running scientific tests. How can they communicate when their hands are occupied? NASA developed wireless headset technology to solve the problem. Now we use wireless headsets with cell phones and other devices.

I See You!

Ever wonder how your map app knows where you are? Orbiting satellites track your every move! Cell phones connect with Global Positioning System (GPS) satellites. These satellites track cell phone locations.

As satellites track your location, you might be using another NASA invention—comfortable shoes! Boots created for the moon landing were made to be comfortable and absorb shock. An ex-NASA engineer took the idea to Nike. *Violà!* Nike Air Trainers were born.

Other companies have mixed NASA's knowledge of special materials with **robotics**. Using NASA comfort foam with robotic technologies, inventors developed better **prosthetics**. These prostheses for people with limb loss are better constructed and more comfortable.

prosthetics (pruhs-THET-iks): the specialty concerned with the design, construction, and fitting of an artificial device to replace a missing or impaired part of the body

robotics (roh-BAH-tiks): technology dealing with the design, construction, and operation of robots

Robot technology is essential to NASA because it sends rovers to planets and moons to collect samples. Rovers use robotic arms to collect these materials. They may need to flip themselves upright if they tumble over. This rover technology was used in the invention of the incredible PackBot. PackBots can search for landmines to keep soldiers safe. They can also take videos and assist in police **reconnaissance**.

reconnaissance (rih-CON-uh-sintz): survey to gain information, especially relating to law enforcement or the military

Rovers also need strong tires to drive over rocks. NASA contracted the Goodyear Tire and Rubber Company to create a solution, and they invented the super-strength parachute cord. The cord is five times stronger than steel. It worked so well that Goodyear began using a similar material in tires. These types of tires are now used around the world.

NASA's newest tire invention is a metal memory tire. It's a hollow metal tire that bounces back to its original shape when it gets bent!

Watch What You're Doing

Imagine an astronaut with a scratched helmet visor. How irritating! NASA invented a scratch-resistant coating to prevent this from happening. Glasses with this coating are ten times more scratch-resistant than normal glasses.

HOT AND COLD

Objects in space can get very hot or very cold! It depends on where the sun is shining. To keep astronauts comfortable, spacecraft use material that reflects sunlight. This thin, heat-reflecting material can also be called a **space blanket**. If the shiny side is wrapped facing your body, it reflects body heat back in. These space blankets are sold in camping stores as survival gear. If you're planning a trip to the mountains, stop by and pick one up!

space blanket (spays BLANG-kit): a light metal-coated sheet designed to retain or reflect heat

Astronauts need extra protection when they're outside a spacecraft. On space walks, the temperature can change by up to 250 degrees Fahrenheit (157 degrees Celcius) in either direction—this problem required NASA to develop special materials for space suits. Space suits use heat- and water-resistant fabric mixed with material from bullet-proof vests! These suits work great for astronauts. Firefighters, the military, and even race car drivers use a similar material.

Don't Blow Your Top

Who would think of using rocket fuel to protect against explosions? The military! Extra rocket fuel is used as a powerful flare to burn through land mines. The mines are destroyed without blowing up.

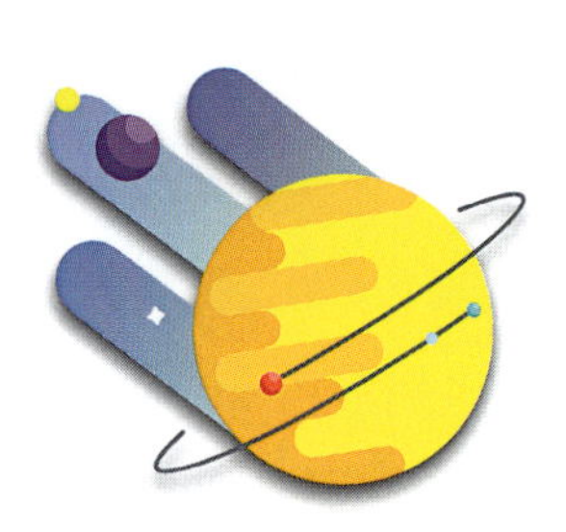

NASA had another problem with heat. When capsules reenter Earth's atmosphere, their temperature can reach 2,700 degrees Fahrenheit (1482 degrees Celcius). Ouch! A campfire is about 1,000 degrees Fahrenheit (538 degrees Celsius). To solve the problem, scientists invented a heat-resistant **ablative** material. It burns off during reentry. Fire retardant paints now also use this technology to prevent fires on airplanes and in buildings. If a fire starts, the paint slows the fire and can even help hold a building together.

ablative(uh-BLAY-tiv): dealing with the removal of material from the surface of an object by vaporization, chipping, or some other erosive process

PREVENTING PROBLEMS

Fire is one of the most dangerous threats in outer space. Astronauts need to know immediately if there is a problem, but they don't want to be bothered by false alarms. To make this possible, NASA developed adjustable smoke detectors. They were used in the USA's first space station, Skylab. Smoke alarms used in our homes today are based on this technology.

Smoke Rises! Or Does It?

Smoke detectors in homes are placed on the ceiling. This is because smoke rises. In outer space with low gravity, heat or smoke can spread in any direction. So, smoke detectors on the *ISS* are placed in the ventilation system that moves the air around.

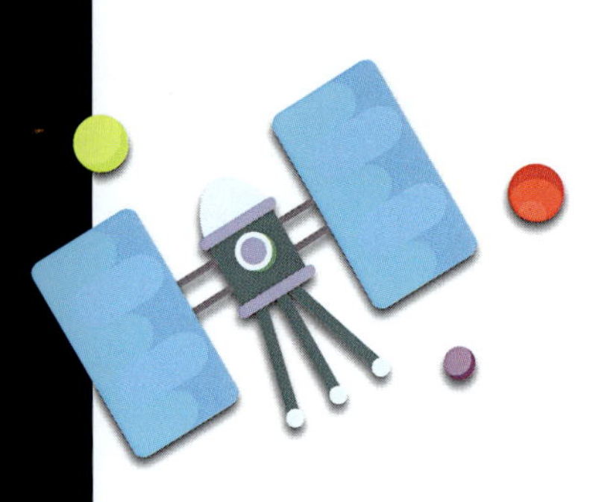

Keeping clean and healthy in space is important. The coronavirus highlighted how quickly a dangerous virus could become. This goes double for space, where bacteria can mutate! The *ISS* tested a new antimicrobial coating called, AGXX®. It dramatically reduced the number of bacteria on contamination-prone surfaces. This type of technology can prevent future problems in spacecraft.

The coronavirus also revealed how difficult it is to be away from family and friends. Or the difficulty of living in a small space for months at a time. But that is what astronauts do.

Alone Time

A trip to Mars would take about six months each way. That's like traveling in an airplane for an entire year just to make one round trip!

FOOD FOR THOUGHT

Astronauts need energy-packed food that doesn't weigh a lot. The original astronauts ate food in cubes or sucked it from tubes. Later, freeze-dried foods improved their diets. Freeze-drying removes the water from food but keeps almost all the nutrients. It can now be found in camping and grocery stores.

The need for a healthy diet also led NASA to add vitamins to food. Where did they find the vitamins? In algae! More accurately, in blue-green, slightly fishy-smelling bacteria. Many baby formulas now use algae-based vitamins. Yum!

Tasty Treats

Freeze-dried ice cream is also called astronaut ice cream. However, there is no evidence that freeze-dried ice cream ever made it into space!

Astronauts also need water. They bring some with them. But most of it comes from recycling every bit of liquid, from sweat to urine! To do this, NASA had to invent an excellent water purification system. Similar systems have made their way back down to Earth to kill bacteria in swimming pools.

These are a few of the amazing ways that space technology positively affects us. In the next twenty years, you'll probably be able to take a trip into space yourself! Until then, look for new space-related inventions and discoveries that improve our everyday lives.

LOUIS STOKES
140 mL

NASA's Mars Perseverance Rover

The Perseverance Rover is ready to bring home to outer space. It is testing advanced technology, preparing for astronauts to live there before 2030. It carried the world's first interplanetary helicopter, called the Ingenuity. It's also looking for signs of ancient life.

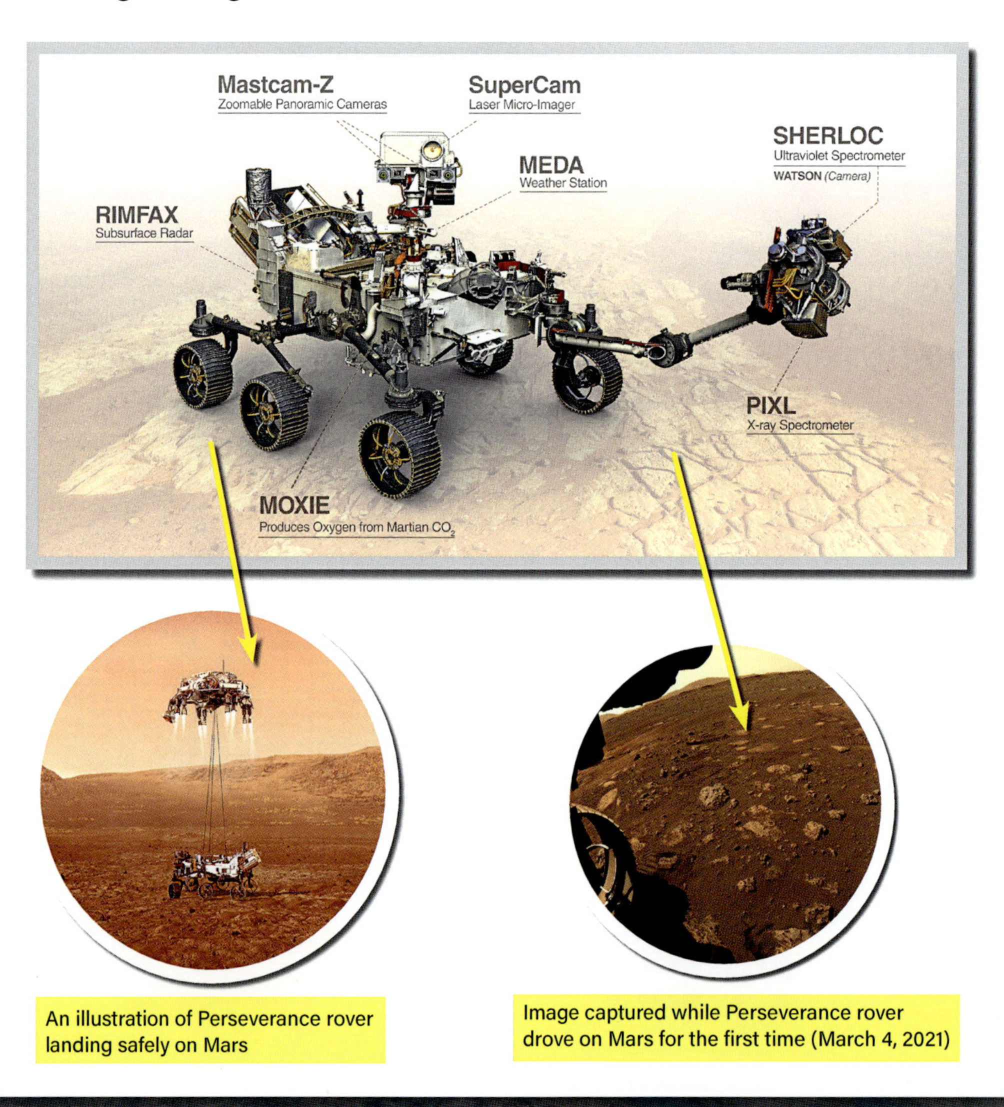

An illustration of Perseverance rover landing safely on Mars

Image captured while Perseverance rover drove on Mars for the first time (March 4, 2021)

Index

cameras 4, 6
freeze-dried food 26
headset 8
ISS 4, 23, 24
NASA 4, 8, 10, 12, 14, 15
PackBot 12
smoke detector 22
space suits 18

After-Reading Questions

1. What space-related inventions do our cell phones use?
2. What two technology improvements were used to make better prosthetics?
3. What does NASA use robotic technology for? What are some ways this technology is used on Earth?
4. How do astronauts get most of their water?
5. What foods can you find in a camping or grocery store that are based on the foods astronauts eat?

Activity

You are on a trip to Mars! Write down at least four things you will need to survive. Now design a place for you and three other astronauts to live in. What inventions or building designs do you need to protect your shelter from high winds, super heat, and icy cold? Draw your shelter, showing at least one of these inventions.

About the Author

Mike Downs is ready to zoom into outer space! But he's waiting for the tickets to get cheap enough to buy. Until then, he'll write about all the amazing inventions that space travel has given us.

www.rourkeeducationalmedia.com

PHOTO CREDITS: Cover: ©3DSculptor/ Getty Images; Cover, 8, 12, 14, 18, 20, 22, 28: ©dem10/ Getty Images; Cover, 1, 3 ,6 ,12 ,14 ,18, 20 ,22 ,24 ,28: ©LineTale/ Shutterstock.com; pages 4- 5: ©Dusan Petkovic/ Shutterstock.com; page 5: ©marco martins/ Shutterstock.com; pages 4-7, 10-11, 16-17, 24-27, 30-31: ©tsuneomp/ Shutterstock.com; page 7: Weekend Images Inc./ Getty Images; pages 8-9: ©BlackJack3D/ Getty Images; pages 10-11: ©andresr/ Getty Images; page 11: ©portishead1/ Getty Images; pages 12-13: ©Greg Sorber/ZUMA Press/Newscom; pages 14-15: Imaging Technology Center at NASA Glenn; pages 14-15: ©Nasa / Legacy Collection/ZUMA Press/Newscom; pages 16-17: ©AMELIE-BENOIST / BSIP/Newscom; pages 18-19: ©Hoch Zwei/ZUMA Press/ Newscom; pages 20-21: ©NASA/Heritage Space/Heritage Images AiWire/Newscom; pages 22-23: ©NASA; page 23: ©svengine/ Getty Images; pages 24-25: ©Nasa/ZUMA Press/Newscom; page 25: ©Nasa/ZUMA Press/Newscom; pages 26-27: ©NASA; page 27: ©Stock Food/Newscom; pages 28-29: ©NASA/ Dominic Hart; page 30: ©NASA/JPL-Caltech

Edited by: Jennifer Doyle
Cover and interior design by: Alison Tracey

Library of Congress PCN Data

Bringing Space Home / Mike Downs
(Reaching for the Stars)
ISBN 978-1-73164-936-2 (hard cover)(alk. paper)
ISBN 978-1-73164-884-6 (soft cover)
ISBN 978-1-73164-988-1 (e-Book)
ISBN 978-1-73165-040-5 (ePub)
Library of Congress Control Number: 2021935273

Rourke Educational Media
Printed in the United States of America
02-0802211948